DEEP
IN THE
DESERT

BY RHONDA LUCAS DONALD

ILLUSTRATED BY SHERRY NEIDIGH

Deep in the Desert

may be sung to "Down in the Valley"

Deep in the desert, down in a mine,
bats are all sleeping, 'til it is time.
Time for the sunset; time to go dine,
bats are all sleeping, 'til it is time.

Bats love the nectar of cactuses tall.
Sip from the flowers; visit them all.
Visit them all, bats; visit them all.
Sip cactus flowers; visit them all.

Bats love the nectar, but don't you know,
cactuses need bats to help them grow.
Flower to flower, pollen they sow.
Cactuses need bats to help them grow.

Deep in the desert, down in a mine,
bats are all sleeping, 'til it is time.
Time for the sunset; time to go dine,
bats are all sleeping, 'til it is time.

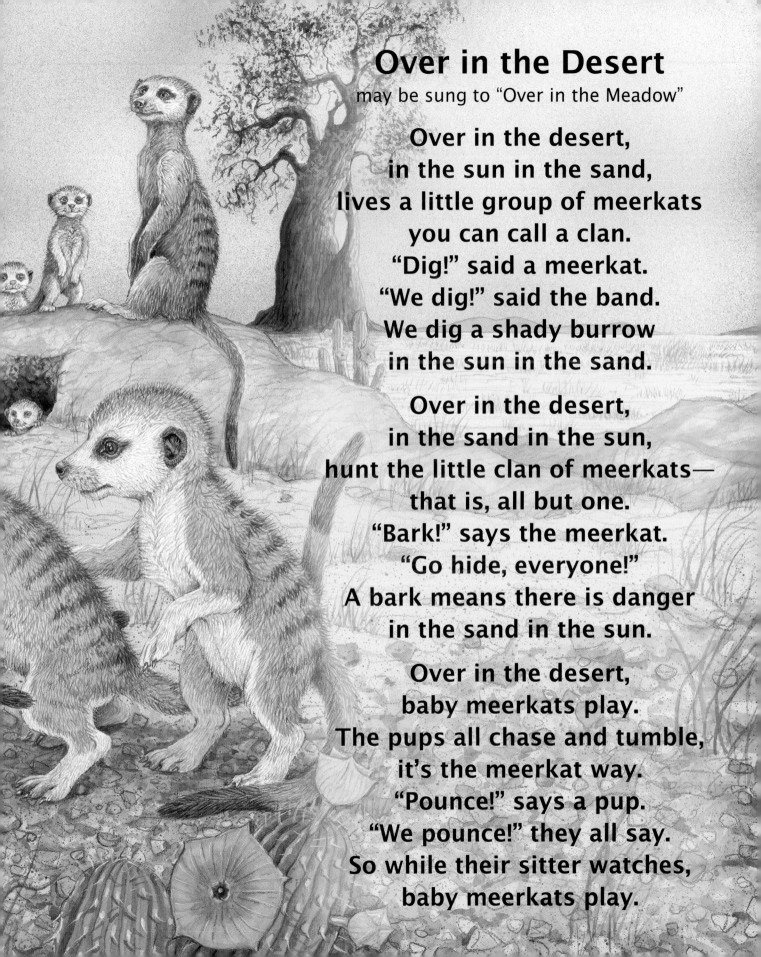

Over in the Desert
may be sung to "Over in the Meadow"

Over in the desert,
in the sun in the sand,
lives a little group of meerkats
you can call a clan.
"Dig!" said a meerkat.
"We dig!" said the band.
We dig a shady burrow
in the sun in the sand.

Over in the desert,
in the sand in the sun,
hunt the little clan of meerkats—
that is, all but one.
"Bark!" says the meerkat.
"Go hide, everyone!"
A bark means there is danger
in the sand in the sun.

Over in the desert,
baby meerkats play.
The pups all chase and tumble,
it's the meerkat way.
"Pounce!" says a pup.
"We pounce!" they all say.
So while their sitter watches,
baby meerkats play.

Desert Tortoise

may be sung to "Baa, Baa, Black Sheep"

Desert tortoise,
may I come inside?
The sun is hot.
I need to hide.

Come in my burrow
for a shady rest.
There is room for everyone,
so please be my guest.

Desert tortoise,
may I come inside?
The sun is hot.
I need to hide.

You're a Fennec Fox

may be sung to "Do Your Ears Hang Low?"

Do you have big ears?
Do they help with what you hear?
Can they turn from side to side?
Can you hear both far and wide?
Do they keep you nice and cool,
like a clear, refreshing pool?
Do you have big ears?

If you do, then . . .

You're a fennec fox.
Dig a den among the rocks.
Sleep inside throughout the day.
Keep the boiling heat at bay.
When the moon and stars come out,
then it's hunting time, no doubt.
You're a fennec fox.

Thorny Devil

may be sung to "Yankee Doodle"

Thorny devil on the sand
soaking up the sun.
Little ant goes marching by;
you eat him just for fun!

Thorny devil on the sand,
why are you so prickly?
Some may think you look a fright
and run off very quickly.

Thorny devil watch your back;
falcon shadow warns.
You tuck your head with little dread—
who'd eat a bunch of thorns?

Thorny devil on the sand,
why are you so prickly?
Some may think you look a fright
and run off very quickly.

Hiss, Gila Monster

may be sung to "Pop, Goes the Weasel"

High atop a desert rock
waits the Gila monster.
A hawk flies by and catches his eye.
Hiss, Gila monster!

Near a nest of Gambel's quail
stalks the Gila monster.
The quail have left their eggs all alone.
Chomp, Gila monster!

Sprawled beneath a prickly pear
lies the Gila monster.
His color's a clue to stay far away.
Poison, Gila monster.

An Odd Birdy That Never Could Fly

may be sung to "There Was an Old Lady Who Swallowed a Fly"

There is an odd birdy that never could fly.
I wonder why the bird cannot fly.
Do you know why?

There is a fast birdy that runs on strong legs.
You can't believe the size of its eggs.
It runs on strong legs because it can't fly.
I wonder why the bird cannot fly.
Do you know why?

There is a tall birdy that's bigger than Dad.
One kick can knock out a lion, it's said.
It kicks with strong legs, although it can't fly.
I wonder why the bird cannot fly.
Do you know why?

There is a big birdy that does a cool dance.
He hopes the girls will give him a chance.
He dances and bows, but he still can't fly.
I wonder why the bird cannot fly.
Do you know why?

This big, running birdy—an ostrich is he.
And flying is simply not his cup of tea.
Now you know why
the birdy can't fly.

The Camel with Two Humps

may be sung to "The Itsy, Bitsy Spider"

The camel with two humps
walks far across the plain.
Where the camel lives
there's hardly any rain.
When the rain does fall,
the camel drinks her fill,
and the camel with two humps
walks far across the hill.

The camel with two humps
has a shaggy coat of fur.
In the winter snow
she really needs it—brrr!
In the summer heat
she sheds it off again.
And the camel with two humps
walks far across the plain.

The camel with two humps
has lashes long and thick.
In the blowing sand,
they really do the trick.
Lashes long and thick
block out the blowing sand,
and the camel with two humps
walks far across the land.

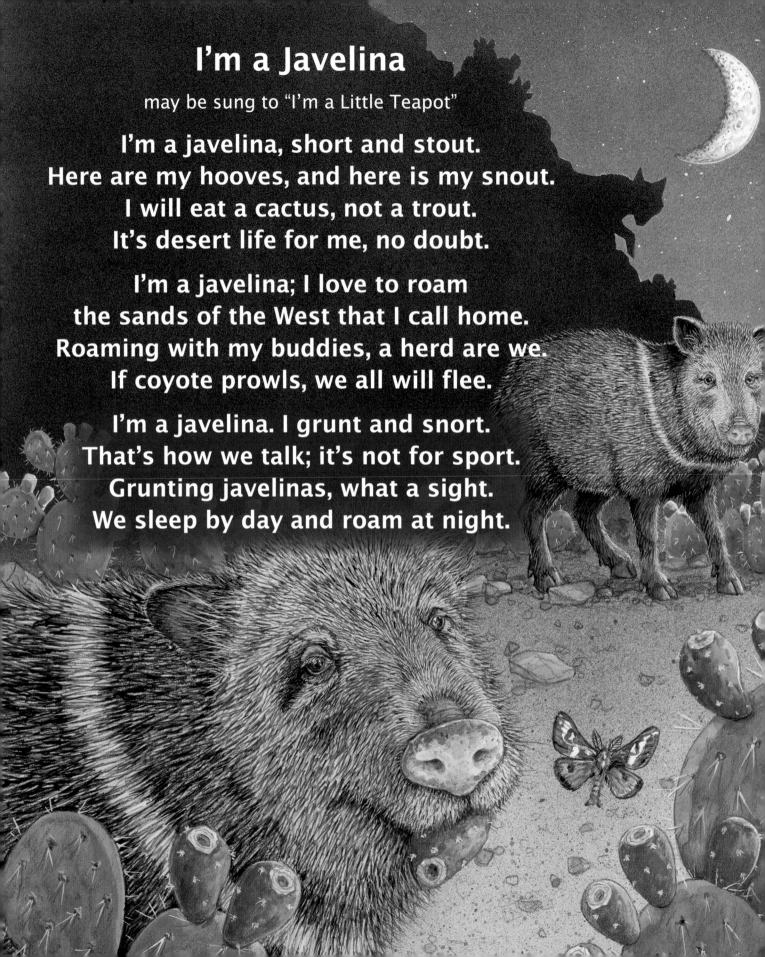

I'm a Javelina

may be sung to "I'm a Little Teapot"

I'm a javelina, short and stout.
Here are my hooves, and here is my snout.
I will eat a cactus, not a trout.
It's desert life for me, no doubt.

I'm a javelina; I love to roam
the sands of the West that I call home.
Roaming with my buddies, a herd are we.
If coyote prowls, we all will flee.

I'm a javelina. I grunt and snort.
That's how we talk; it's not for sport.
Grunting javelinas, what a sight.
We sleep by day and roam at night.

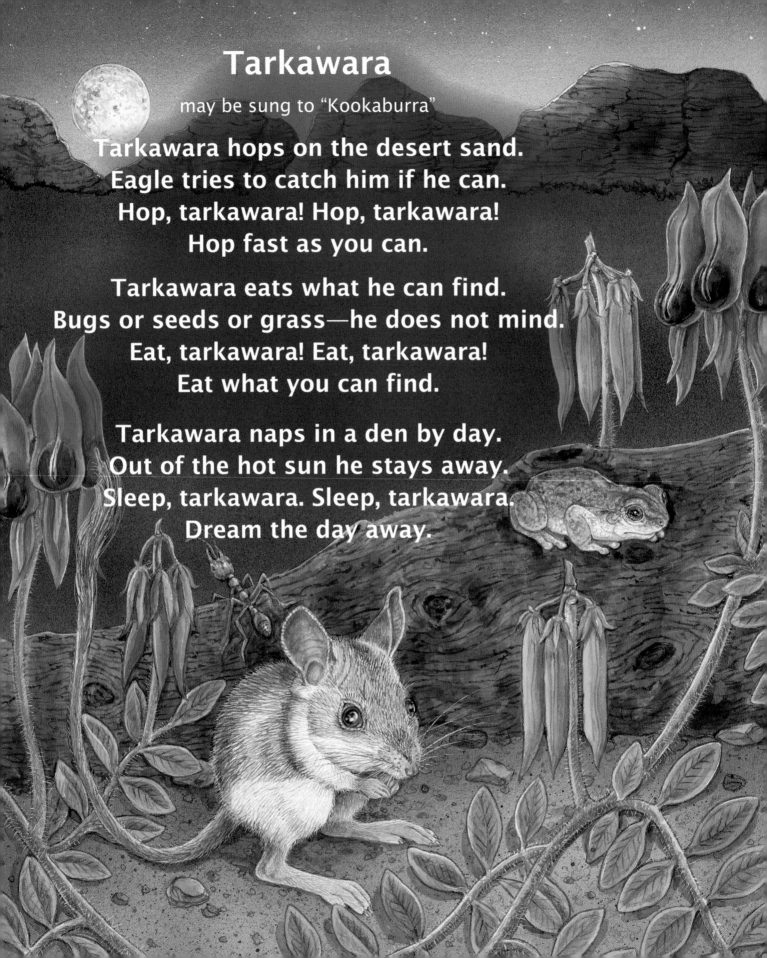

Tarkawara

may be sung to "Kookaburra"

Tarkawara hops on the desert sand.
Eagle tries to catch him if he can.
Hop, tarkawara! Hop, tarkawara!
Hop fast as you can.

Tarkawara eats what he can find.
Bugs or seeds or grass—he does not mind.
Eat, tarkawara! Eat, tarkawara!
Eat what you can find.

Tarkawara naps in a den by day.
Out of the hot sun he stays away.
Sleep, tarkawara. Sleep, tarkawara.
Dream the day away.

Out in the Desert

may be sung to "Over the River"

Out in the desert it's dry and hot,
but cactuses grow tall.
Without any leaves, they don't seem to need
to have them after all—aw!

Out in the desert it's dry and hot,
and cactuses have spikes.
They get in the way, keep critters at bay.
They get too close it hurts—yikes!

Out in the desert it's dry and hot,
but cactuses are food
to bugs and to birds and even to herds
of bighorn sheep, it's true—ooo!

Out in the desert it's dry and hot,
and cactuses stand high.
They cover the land and hold down the sand
and reach up to the sky.

Out Here in the Desert

may be sung to "On Top of Old Smokey"

Out here in the desert, it's dusty and dry.
Life's tough in the desert, and that is no lie.

Sometimes in the desert, it's blistering hot.
And sometimes it's freezing. I'm kidding you not.

If you think the desert is lifeless, you're wrong.
There're all sorts of creatures that call it a home.

There're snakes, bats, and beetles; there're lizards and birds.
There're big hairy spiders and deer found in herds.

So if you should go to the desert to roam,
be kind to the place that so many call home.

For Creative Minds

The Desert Habitat

Some deserts are hot, and some are cold, but the one thing that all deserts have in common is that they are dry. On average, a desert gets less than 10 to 12 inches (25-30 cm) of rain a year. Some do not even get that much. The driest place on Earth, the Atacama Desert in South America has areas that haven't seen any rain in 400 years!

Hot (tropical or subtropical) deserts are warm throughout the year, but very hot in the summer. Temperatures drop at night to cool or cold. Rain comes in short bursts any time of the year and may even evaporate before it hits the ground. There are long, dry periods in between rain showers. The Chihuahan, Sonoran, and Mojave Deserts in Mexico and the American Southwest are hot deserts. The Sahara and Kalahari Deserts in Africa are also hot.

Polar deserts have long, cold winters and can have snow- or ice-covered ground. Antarctica and parts of Arctic Europe and North America are polar deserts.

Coastal deserts are found along continental coasts and have salty soils or sand. They generally have cool winters (with whatever rain there may be) and long, warm, dry summers. The Atacama in South America (Chile) and the Namib in Africa are coastal deserts.

Cold winter deserts (also called semi-arid deserts) have cold winters with some snow and long, dry, hot summers. Many are formed by a "rain shadow effect," which is when high mountains block precipitation from reaching the area. The Great Basin Desert in Utah and Montana and the Gobi Desert in Asia are cold winter deserts.

Desert Fun Facts

Cacti can hold water in their stems (trunks). The spines (leaves) protect the plant from animals and break up airflow, helping the cacti to hold water.

Lesser long-nosed bats depend on cacti (and agaves) for food. The bats spread the cacti's pollen to help the plants grow. The cacti bloom at night so the nocturnal bats can find them!

One meerkat acts as guard while the rest of the clan hunts or plays. The guard barks a warning to let the group know to run to their burrow.

When scared, thorny devils tuck their heads and show a fake head. They can also change color to match the dirt.

Gila monsters have bright colors to warn animals that they are poisonous. We use this poison in a medicine to treat diabetes.

Many desert animals spend their days hiding from the hot sun in burrows dug by desert tortoises.

Male ostriches can be 9 feet (2.7 m) tall! They dance (bow, wave their wings, and bob up and down) to attract females. Ostrich eggs are about the size of a small cantaloupe.

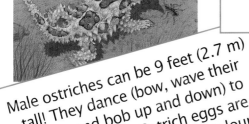

Javelinas, also called collared peccaries, have a ring of light-colored fur around their necks that looks a bit like a collar.

Deserts of the World

Use the map on the next page to find the location or answer the following questions. Answers are upside down at the bottom of this page. Older children should identify animal locations with grid coordinates.

1. On what continent is the Sahara Desert?
2. In which desert do Bactrian camels live?
3. In which desert do fennec foxes live?
4. On what continent do tarkawaras and thorny devils live?
5. On what continent do lesser long-nosed bats and Gila monsters live?

Answers: 1) Africa; 2) Gobi 2,M; 3) Sahara 4,I; 4) Australia; 5) North America

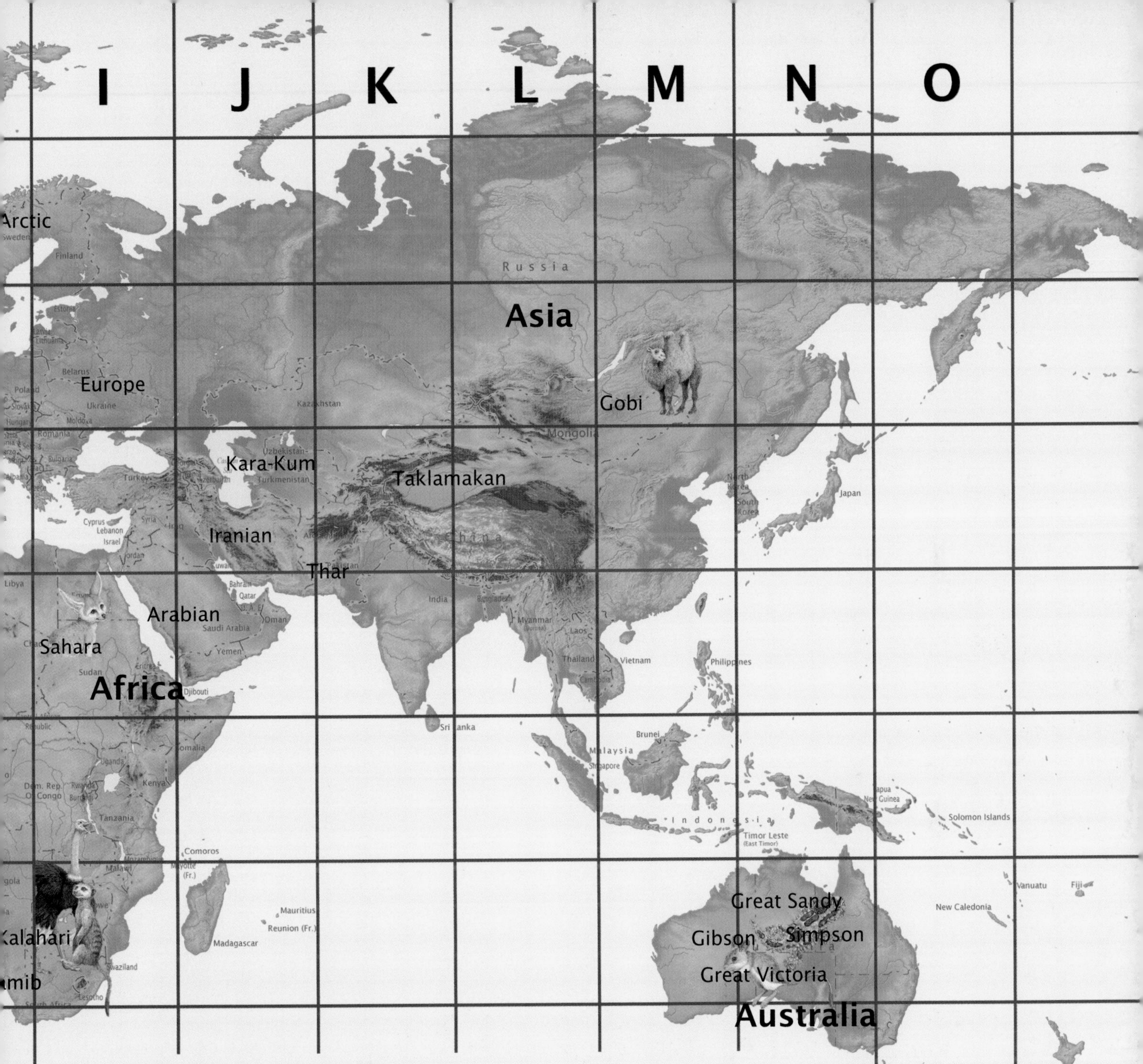

I J K L M N O

Arctic

Russia

Asia

Europe

Gobi

Kara-Kum

Taklamakan

Iranian

Thar

Arabian

Sahara

Africa

Kalahari

Namib

Great Sandy

Gibson   Simpson

Great Victoria

Australia

Deserts are on all seven continents including Antarctica!

Find some of the animals that live in the world's deserts.

Older children can identify where the animal is by grid number,
by continent, or the desert in which the animal lives.

Antarctica
Antarctica Desert

Match the Desert Adaptations

Plants and animals that live in the desert have special body parts or behaviors (adaptations) that help them survive without very much water. Those living things that live in hot, tropical deserts have to protect themselves from the sun too. Match the plant or animal adaptations. Answers are upside down at the bottom of the page.

1 My humps store fat to give me energy when I can't find food. I can go several days without drinking water, but when I do find water, I can drink gallons in minutes. I can close my nostrils so sand doesn't blow up my nose. Bushy eyebrows and two rows of eyelashes keep sand out of my eyes.

2 I get water from eating prickly pear cactuses (spines and all) that most other animals can't eat. I hunt early in the morning and in the evening (crepuscular) when it is cool. If it gets too hot, I'll just hunt at night.

3 I get most of the water I need from the plants I eat. I spend most of my time living in my underground burrow where it is cool. If it gets too hot in the summer, I go into a deep sleep—like summer hibernation (aestivation).

4 My huge ears help to keep me cool like "air conditioners." I have fur on the bottom of my feet so the hot desert sand doesn't burn me. I sleep all day and am up at night (nocturnal) when it is cooler. I am similar to the kit fox found in the deserts of the American Southwest.

5 I store fat and water in my thick tail and can go months between meals. In fact, I only eat three or four times a year. I spend most of my time in my underground burrow. My bright colors let other animals know that I am poisonous.

6 I sleep in a deep, dark cave, mineshaft, or even in trees or cracks in rocks during the hot day. I come out at night (nocturnal) when it is cool. My very long tongue helps me to reach deep into cactus flowers to sip the nectar that I need to eat.

lesser long-nose bat   javelina   desert tortoise   Gila monster   fennec fox   Bactrian camel

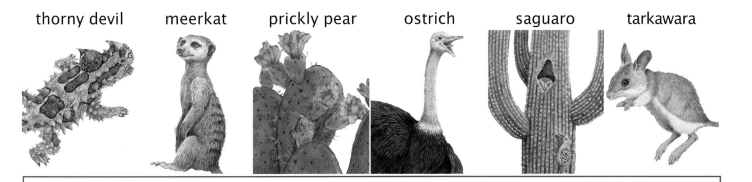

thorny devil	meerkat	prickly pear	ostrich	saguaro	tarkawara

7 I store water in long, flat, green stem "pads" and protect those pads with sharp spines. I grow low to the ground to help conserve any moisture I can find.

8 My ears close to keep sand out and the dark patches around my eyes cut down the Sun's glare so I can see.

9 Ridges between the thorns along my back carry rainwater and dew to my mouth. If it gets too hot during the day, I use my claws to dig a shallow burrow, or I find shade under a plant. I am similar to horned lizards found in the western part of the North American continent.

10 I sleep with my family in a one-room burrow during the day (nocturnal). I get most of my water from the seeds that I eat, but I will also travel for long distances to find rain. I am similar to the kangaroo rat in the Mexican and American deserts and the jerboa in Africa and Asia.

11 Like many types of cacti, I store water in my fleshy stems and have spines to protect them. My roots aren't deep, but they are very long to catch as much water as possible when it rains. My roots can be as long as I am tall!

12 Like many desert-living animals, I can go for several days without drinking anything. If I do find water, I like to take a bath! My very long legs help me to see danger coming so I can run away—and I can run very fast! I can even kick a lion if I have to!

For Bruce, my oasis, who makes life anything but dry—RLD

To my sister, Sandy—SN

Thanks to Lisa Evans, Education Specialist, and Kelly Holler, Visitor Use Assistant, Amistad National Recreation Area and David Elkowitz, Chief of Interpretation, Big Bend National Park Rio Grande Wild and Scenic River for verifying the desert information in this book.

Thanks to Laura Scoble for reviewing the songs' sheet music, which can be found in the online teaching activities. Go to www.ArbordalePublishing.com and click on the book's cover.

Library of Congress Cataloging-in-Publication Data

Donald, Rhonda Lucas, 1962-
  Deep in the desert / by Rhonda Lucas Donald ; illustrated by Sherry Neidigh.
    p. cm.
  ISBN 978-1-60718-125-5 (hardback) -- ISBN 978-1-60718-135-4 (pbk.) -- ISBN 978-1-60718-145-3 (english ebook) -- ISBN 978-1-60718-155-2 (spanish ebook) 1. Desert ecology--Juvenile literature. 2. Desert animals--Juvenile literature. 3. Children's songs--Juvenile literature. I. Neidigh, Sherry, ill. II. Title.
  QH541.5.D4D66 2011
  577.54--dc22
                              2010049625

Interest level: 003-008
Grade level: P-3
ATOS™ Level: 3.0
Lexile Level: 500 Lexile Code: AD

Also available as eBooks featuring auto-flip, auto-read, 3D-page-curling, and selectable English and Spanish text and audio

Keywords: adaptations, climate, compare/contrast: plants/animals, coordinate grid, geography, habitat (desert), landforms (desert), life science, map, nursery rhymes, repeated lines, rhythm or rhyme

Manufactured in China, May 2016
This product conforms to CPSIA 2008
Second Printing

Arbordale Publishing
formerly Sylvan Dell Publishing
Mt. Pleasant, SC 29464
www.ArbordalePublishing.com